The Girl From Over There

The Hopeful Story of a Young Jewish Immigrant

Sky Pony Press books may be purchased in bulk at special discounts for sales promotion, corporate gifts, fund-raising, or educational purposes. Special editions can also be created to specifications. For details, contact the Special Sales Department, Sky Pony Press, 307 West 36th Street, 11th Floor, New York, NY 10018 or info@skyhorsepublishing.com.

Sky Pony® is a registered trademark of Skyhorse Publishing, Inc.®, a Delaware corporation.

Visit our website at www.skyhorsepublishing.com.

10 9 8 7 6 5 4 3 2 1

Library of Congress Cataloging-in-Publication Data is available on file.

Cover design by Kai Texel

Print ISBN: 978-1-5107-5367-9
Ebook ISBN: 978-1-5107-5368-6

Printed in China

The Girl From Over There

The Hopeful Story of a Young Jewish Immigrant

Sharon Rechter
Illustrated by Karla Gerard

Sky Pony Press
New York

In honor of my grandparents the beloved
Meir & Irena Rechter, and Blanka & David Lavie
who were the inspiration for this book.

Chapter 1

We were sitting on the big lawn, making plans for the upcoming Hanukkah party, when she popped up from behind the rosebushes. She seemed unsure about whether she should come out of her hiding spot, but once she realized we were all looking at her she came out. Two long, black braids framed a frightened face with big brown eyes. She looked about our age, eleven or so, and she was clutching a tattered, purple teddy bear to her chest. She stood up straight, and though a fiery sort of bravery burned in her eyes, there was fear in them too. Her old dress, once white, was now gray from grime and wear.

As she stood there, we—the children of the kibbutz[1]—stared at her in wonder, puzzled by her disheveled dress and, given her age, the faded teddy bear in her hands. She looked at us, too afraid to come any closer, so we simply sat there, judging, aiming somewhat condescending looks at her appearance, which was both confusing and amusing at the same time.

She kept her frightened eyes fixed on us for another minute or two.

I wondered, *Did she want us to invite her to join us? Or was she scared of us?*

Then, in a flash, she ran for her life. We immediately abandoned our party preparations and began to chatter among ourselves. Who was she? Where had she come from? Would she stay? Her clothes were so weird; where were they from? Was she from *over there*? We'd heard, after all, that barely any children had made it from over there.

---

1   A kibbutz is a collective settlement in Israel where groups of people live and work together, prevalent in the 1900s. The goal of a kibbutz was to create an independent community based on equality, social justice, and the sharing of property. Kibbutzniks—the people who lived in a kibbutz—did not own any possessions of their own, even clothing. Any gifts or money a member received from outside the kibbutz were automatically placed in a community fund for everyone. Children lived separately from adults in a shared "children's house" where they spent their time learning, playing, and sleeping. Parents spent about three to four hours a day with their children after they finished their work and before they had dinner.

Was she alone? Where were her parents? Did Leah, the caretaker,[2] know about her? She was new. That much we knew for sure.

We hated her instantly, but no one could say why. She was just different, and she didn't belong. What kind of a girl wore a dress on the kibbutz, and a dress like that one, so narrow and worn-out? And who, at our age, still carried around a stuffed animal? Maybe that was why she seemed so different to us.

Our thoughts were cut short by Joel, who called us to the dining hall.

Even though we were a small kibbutz, at lunchtime our dining hall was bustling with children, families, toddlers, all speaking at once, creating a loud mix of laughter and heated discussions about daily news and kibbutz gossip. And since it was my turn to serve food to the kibbutz members, the new girl completely slipped my mind.

After lunch, the other members returned to their duties, and I stayed behind to clean up and clear the

---

2   The caretaker was responsible for taking care of all the children in the kibbutz. She supervised them in the communal children's house, made sure they were fed, clothed, and ready for bed on time, and took charge of their education.

tables with Abigail, Yael, and Gili, the other girls on dining hall duty that day. Naturally, our conversation found its way back to the girl we had seen that morning.

"Did you see her?" Gili asked.

"See who?" Yael replied.

"The girl with the teddy bear."

"Of course I did," I said.

"So, what do you think about her?" Gili asked condescendingly.

"I think she wanted to sit with us," Abigail said.

Then Gili added, "I bet she's from *over there*."

"Why do they keep sending them all here, to our kibbutz?" Yael asked resentfully.

"She's probably all alone," I pondered out loud.

Abigail asked mockingly, "So, Michal? Do you feel sorry for her?"

"No way," I said, snapping out of my daydream. To emphasize this, I added, "As far as I'm concerned, she can go to hell!"

"You know, they say they're different," Gili added.

"What do you mean *different*?" I asked, as if trying to find the reason I felt so disgusted by her.

"Oh, please," Yael said. "Can't you tell? They're so weird."

She made a face as she said this, sending a wave of laughter through us.

"All of them?" asked Abigail.

"Yes," Yael said knowingly. "They're all the same. They're cowards, and they're weird, and they hold on to old things like some precious treasure. And they always hold back their tears like heroes."

"Shh," Gili whispered. "Leah's coming over with her."

We fell silent and turned back to our work. Leah opened the door. "Hello, girls," she said kindly.

"Hello," we answered in a chorus.

"Girls, this is Miriam. She's new to the kibbutz, and she's come to us from far away. Let's make sure she's happy here with us."

An awkward chuckle rippled through our group.

Leah walked over to me. "Michal, dear, is there anything left to eat?" she asked.

"Yes," I answered. "It's all in the kitchen."

Leah walked into the kitchen, leaving behind the frightened girl with the teddy bear in her arms. We all turned to stare at her.

Abigail whispered to me, "She doesn't look that weird or different to me. Maybe she is a little bit . . ." Abigail was searching for the right word when Yael cut her off.

"Would you like to see a rabbit?" Yael teased, her eyes glancing back and forth between us and the skinny new girl, who was ready to retreat at any moment.

Without waiting for an answer, Yael walked up to her and asked, "Are you from over there?"

The girl said nothing.

"Are you from over there?" Yael repeated her question with force.

"She's not answering," Abigail said. "Leave her alone."

"She'll answer me," Yael cried out, and pulled hard on Miriam's braid.

Miriam gasped in pain, her eyes pleading. But she did not open her mouth.

"You see, I told you. They hold back their tears like heroes and act like they're all perfect," Yael said, proud of herself. She let go of the girl's braid. Free of Yael's grasp, she fled. Unsettled by Yael, we returned to our jobs in silence.

A few minutes later, Leah stepped out of the kitchen and asked, "Girls, where is she?"

"She left," Yael said. An evil glint burned in our eyes.

Chapter 2

That evening, Leah walked Miriam to our communal bedroom.[3] There she was, the "weird girl," still clutching her ever-present teddy bear.

Abigail, Gili, Yael, and I exchanged quick glances. We were scared that Miriam had told Leah about what had happened in the dining hall, and we braced ourselves for our punishment. But Leah didn't say a word about it. Was it possible she'd decided to ignore it? Or maybe . . . maybe she knew nothing about it.

Leah spoke in her motherly tone and said, "Girls, I'd like you to meet Miriam. She came here all the way from Poland. Miriam is an orphan; she has no mother and no father—just a little brother, who is five years old."

---

3 Until the 1980s, kibbutz children were raised mostly apart from their parents. As part of this arrangement, the children of the kibbutz all slept together in one large, shared bedroom inside the children's house.

Gili whispered to me, "You see? She *is* from over there!"

"Please make her feel welcome," Leah continued.

"Oh, we will!" Yael muttered, and I smiled.

"She's been through a terrible war. I know there might be times when you think she's a bit odd." Hearing this, Abigail giggled, trying to hide her smile behind my back. "But you must understand, children, that she's just going through a difficult time. This is a new place, with a different language, and her memories are very painful."

Leah proceeded to tell us about the horrific war that had just ended in Europe and the Nazi persecution of the Jews. We weren't listening, as it seemed so far away. We'd heard these things before from immigrants, both legal and illegal.[4] Nathan, who'd arrived just a few weeks ago, would tell all the children his story every chance he got. But, to be honest, we had yet to meet a girl from over there.

---

4   After the Nazis were defeated at the end of World War II, many surviving Jews left Europe to build new lives for themselves elsewhere. As many as 170,000 displaced Jewish people immigrated to Israel during the first several years after the war, some of whom—having no family or resources left of their own—sought comfort in the kibbutzim. Some people went to their new countries legally, meaning the governments involved gave them paperwork that allowed them to be there. Other people couldn't get this paperwork, so they "snuck in" illegally.

Leah finished her introduction and showed Miriam to her new bed. Our stares were so aggressive—so menacing—as we watched her that I'm sure she must've felt it.

Leah placed Miriam's meager personal belongings, which were packed in a loose bundle, into a wooden cubby. *Is that really all of her stuff?*, I wondered. They exchanged a few words; Leah spoke, and Miriam nodded. When she was done, Leah stood up straight, looked at us, and said, "Miriam only knows a few words in Hebrew, and will need some help, so I would like to ask one of you . . ." Leah paused. It was as if she was measuring the room, seeking a pair of kind eyes, a glimpse of generosity, but she didn't find it. All eyes were avoiding her, focused on an unseen mark on the floor. She continued, asking someone to please help Miriam. Her voice was assertive, yet I could now hear some disappointment in it, too.

Leah continued to look around, a frown on her face as she waited, but the room was deadly silent. No one wanted to volunteer.

Suddenly, Dan took a single step toward them, saying, "I'll help her."

His eyes were kind, his voice warm. I felt a pinch in my heart.

It was then that I noticed that Dan's bed was right

across from Miriam's bed, and I felt my anger toward Miriam bubble up once again. Dan was *my* boyfriend. I was suddenly afraid she'd take my place with him, and at that moment I justified Yael's cruel prank and even took pride in it.

I can't remember the rest of that night. I was so anxious about the "new girl" that I paid no attention to anything else around me. I'm sure the other kids eventually got into their beds, and Leah turned out the lights, just like normal, but I honestly have no memory of it. I was so worried that I couldn't sleep all night.

The next day, just as I expected, Miriam became the center of attention at the kibbutz; the grown-ups fretted over her, brought her gifts and candy, and peppered her with question after question, just in case she knew anything about the fate of their missing loved ones. In reality, Miriam knew very little. But the worst thing about that day was Dan, who never left her side and offered her his help at every moment.

I was consumed by hate. *I won't let her do this*, I thought to myself. *She will not take my place.* I was already planning the cruelest prank I could possibly imagine: I would steal away her purple teddy bear, this strange friend of hers that she apparently loved with all her heart. Maybe she'd gotten it from her parents.

The day passed slowly. I tried to stay away from everybody—most of all from her. I found comfort in working out the smallest details of my plan—without saying a word about it to anyone else, of course.

That night, when we climbed into our beds, I waited for everyone else to fall asleep. Then, I approached her bed. Like me, she was still awake and seemed worried. As always, she was ready to run. Even in the darkness, I noticed the flicker of fear in her eyes as she saw me coming closer. The teddy bear was clutched tightly in her arms. I grabbed it with force. Not immediately understanding my malicious intentions, she stayed put. But soon, she figured out what I was up to and panicked. Tears shone in her eyes. She jumped off her bed and leapt toward her teddy bear to grab it back. So I pulled it toward me—and she pulled it toward her. A few seconds later, the faded cloth tore, and the bear's insides—chunks of sponge and moldy rags—scattered at the foot of the bed. Seeing this, I defiantly tossed away the teddy bear's leg, which I'd still had in my hand. With an evil smile on my lips, I walked back to my bed, my back straight and tall. "That should teach her a lesson," I whispered to myself.

I curled up in my blanket. In the night's silence, I heard her muffled crying as she gathered up the pieces, making sure not to lose a single one, as if she were collecting a set of precious pearls. When she finally finished, she went back to bed. Her soft sobbing continued for a while longer, and suddenly it gave me the most awful feeling.

Chapter 3

At dawn, Leah came in to wake everyone up.

"Good morning," she said cheerfully, moving from bed to bed, smiling and helping us out of our blankets. She walked over to Miriam's bed. Miriam's eyes were furious—thundering, even. Leah looked around, and her gaze fell on the shredded teddy bear. She was astonished but said nothing. The two of them looked at each other.

Their silence said more than words ever could.

Leah was born in Poland as well, and she too probably came to Israel as a child. But this hadn't been during the war, she once told us, so she hadn't suffered or lived through the same horrors that many of the other members had.

They whispered to each other. Leah promised Miriam she'd sew it up. She even promised her a brand-new teddy bear, and she hugged the gaunt little girl. The rage in her eyes died down. Miriam felt safe in Leah's warm arms.

Suddenly, Leah snapped up and asked, "Alright, children, who's the big hero?" Her tone was angry with a touch of mockery. No one answered.

"Who tore up the teddy bear?" Leah asked, growing angrier. I was sure everyone knew it was me, but no one said a word. That was how we were at the kibbutz: we didn't rat on each other!

"What teddy bear?" asked Yael, feigning innocence. We all went silent again. No one made a sound. And then Dan raised his hand. We were all stunned. I was overcome with worry. Dan's hand held up high made me anxious. Would he tell on me?

Leah turned to him and asked, "Yes, Dan?"

"No . . . nothing," he said, awkwardly.

I let out a sigh of relief. But my joy did not last long.

Leah asked again, this time quieter, "Who did this?"

Getting no answers out of us once more, she called me over, to my astonishment, while rushing the others off to the washroom. Everybody else left. Yael winked at me and disappeared as well.

Miriam sat on her bed and looked at Leah helplessly.

Dan walked over to her. He tried to gesture something

to her with his hands and wound up looking pretty silly. I did my best to hide the smile on my lips, but I couldn't quite do it. Where I failed, he succeeded by shooting an angry glance at me that froze the smile on my face.

After failing miserably at sign language, Dan took Miriam by the hand and together they marched off to the washroom. Leah followed them with her eyes, a kind smile spreading on her lips.

The preaching I received on how a leader like me should put more effort in to welcoming a new kid was not as bad as I expected. Much worse was what happened with the others after they had left. After Leah scolded me, I walked down to the dining hall. I sat in the middle of the bench, where none of the other girls from my class dared to sit, and Yael told me all about what happened in the washroom.

When the new couple reached the communal washroom, Dvora and Rachel, the women in charge there, were alarmed by the sight of the neglected girl and stared at her in wonder while the other children hurried off to stand in line for one of the three bathrooms stalls.

When they were done, they quickly grabbed their toothbrushes, their toothpaste, and their personal towels and rushed to stand in line for the sink. Dvora whispered

in Rachel's ear. We heard fragments of their conversation—said Yael—words like "over there," "new," and "alone." Then, Dvora walked over to the cupboard and pulled out a toothbrush and a fresh, clean towel. She turned to the girl, who seemed frightened by the commotion around her, and handed her the toiletries. The girl recoiled and seemed to be looking for a way out. Dvora, who was impatient that morning, gave up immediately and passed the task on to Rachel. Rachel walked up to Miriam, a motherly smile on her face. She tried to complete the task Dvora had abandoned, and she was indeed successful. Miriam took what was offered to her with shaking hands. Her voice was filled with wonder and hoarse with excitement as she blurted out, "*Moje?*" (Mine?) Dan tried to decipher the meaning of the word. "It's probably Polish," he said to Dvora, who nodded.

Dan led Miriam to the sink and showed her how to use the toothbrush and toothpaste she'd just received. Rachel, who noticed the bond of friendship forming between the two of them, sent them to the storage room to get Miriam her new clothes. The two left the washroom holding hands.

I was fuming as Yael told her story. I listened closely, trying to extract even the tiniest detail that may have slipped her mind. In the background, I could hear the boys' table growing increasingly noisy as they began singing songs and cheering each other on. It was strange, but the girls' table always seemed so much quieter, most of us preferring simple chatter and gossip to rowdy behavior. The boys, on the other hand, were wilder, often dancing and joking around. In fact, the only time we ever invited a boy to our table was if he had some new bit of gossip to share with us; stories about a couple caught out in the orchard, for instance, a new illegal immigrant, or some other interesting news. They were known as "the gang." I looked over at their table. Dan's seat was empty, and Rami and Doron were gone too. I looked around for Dan, and suddenly noticed Rami and Doron standing in the doorway.

I got up from the bench. Yael and Gili, my "entourage," scraped their chairs along the floor, intending to join me, but I gestured with a finger that I wanted to be left alone. I walked over to the two boys.

"Hi," I said.

"Hi," they replied.

"Have you seen Dan?"

"Don't you mean, have we seen the new couple?" they said, mocking.

I didn't need any more than that to get the hint. Had things gone this far already? My heart was beating fast now. I imagined its pounding could be heard in the entire dining hall.

The boys looked at me, gloating silently.

I turned to look at the door again, hoping for a savior, and just then, it opened wide. Dan walked in, and Doron and Rami stared at him in surprise. He was with her, and she was dressed the same as the rest of us, the children of the kibbutz. I was stunned. She looked just like one of us now.

Dan came up to me, while she, seeing me, lingered behind as if rooted to the floor. I expected Dan to say words of affection and apology, but instead he said, "Michal, I'm so glad I ran into you. Who are you waiting for? Are you done eating?" Without waiting for my answer, he added, "Would you mind letting Miriam join your table? It's just, you know, I volunteered." He shrugged helplessly.

"Dan," I said. "I want us to talk."

"Me, too," he replied. "But I'm starving. Would you mind putting it off till later?"

"Not at all," I said. Under my breath, I added bitterly, "Nothing I would rather do, your royal highness. . . ."

Dan smiled gratefully and disappeared among his

friends. I didn't know if I was sad or relieved that he couldn't see how I really felt.

I pulled on Miriam's arm until we were out of his sight, and then I let go of her and went back to my seat. I smiled. I knew exactly who would go get her. I slid my dessert toward Abigail and said, "Go get her." This was all I had to say. Abigail got the hint. She rose heavily and, with obvious reluctance, walked over to Miriam. For every step Abigail took, Miriam took half a step backwards.

At this point, Leah walked into the dining hall. She noticed Miriam looking anxious and approached her. She took her arm gently, exchanged a few words and smiles with her, and signaled Abigail to return to her seat. Leah sat Miriam down at the far corner of the long table. I took back the sweet dessert from Abigail, who hid her anger with a mischievous smile. I took pleasure in my dessert, and caught an occasional glimpse from afar of Dan, his friends, and Miriam, who'd once again attracted a crowd of a few grown-ups.

The sight filled me with rage. I thought to myself, *Enough already, Dan!* I swallowed my pride and shot up from the bench, rushing to his table with wide, quick strides. But then, as if only to make me angry, someone beat me to it. It was Leah.

"Dan," she said. "Would you mind coming with me?"

"Sure," he said.

And I was forced to leave with my tail between my legs. "What does she have to say that's so important?" I grumbled. I returned to my seat in a foul mood. "What happened?" asked Yael, while all the other girls huddled around us.

"Why don't you leave me alone?" I yelled. "It's my life, not yours!"

I left the table and headed back to my room. On my way out, I noticed Dan and Leah sitting on the dining hall steps.

I hid behind the door and listened in.

Leah was speaking. "Dan, you are a brave boy, and I appreciate your behavior."

Dan seemed surprised. He thought to himself, *All this because I didn't dare admit this morning that I ripped apart the teddy bear?*

Leah saw the confusion on his face, and as if reading his thoughts, she laughed and said, "Oh, silly! I know you had nothing to do with it."

His blue eyes expressed bewilderment. The question mark on his face was easy to read. *What does she know?* he wondered to himself.

"Miriam told me all about you, and how without your help she wouldn't have been able to handle the other children. So, it makes absolutely no sense that it would have been you!"

"Leah, do you know who it was?" Dan asked. Guilt, but also relief, filled his heart.

"Yes," she said, her voice tinged with sadness.

"You know, I actually like Miriam," Dan said suddenly, as if trying to change the subject. "Is her brother having a hard time, too?"

"Not as much," she replied. Sadness mixed with joy in the smile on her lips, as if she was remembering something. "He's made new friends already and has no resistance to the new clothes. You saw how hard it was to get Miriam to wear our clothes. You were the only one who could get her to do it." After a moment she added, "There are hardly any differences between him and the other children. He's doing his best to fit in with them."

"Can I visit him?" Dan asked, pleading.

Leah glanced at her watch. "You won't have any time to eat."

"That's okay, I can go one day without olives and cheese," said Dan.

"Your mother would disagree."

He nodded with a smile. "You're like a friend," he said to her.

She smiled. They got up from the steps and walked over to the toddlers' room.

A small boy with a head of black curls ran across the room. "There he is," said Leah. The boy sat down on the floor and started playing with building blocks with Sarah and David, Dan's little twin brother and sister. The twins were surprised to see their older brother and squealed with joy. Dan picked them up in his arms. Then he remembered the reason for his visit, and asked Leah the little boy's name, who was now clinging to her legs.

"Over there his name was Moses, and here in Israel we'll call him Moshe, of course."

"Poor little guy. He'll grow up and won't remember his parents," Dan said sadly.

"That's true. But think about the advantage he has in being so young, Dan."

"What advantage?" he asked.

"Miriam would feel hurt if her friends abandoned her in the middle of the game, but he, well, look at him— your brother and sister stopped playing with him, and he's already found new friends. He has his whole life ahead of him, and soon he'll forget the bad experiences."

Dan looked around, as if searching for something. He spotted a ball in the corner of the room and walked over to pick it up. Carefully, he tossed it to Moshe. The toddler caught the ball and tried to throw it back at Dan. Dan chuckled at the sight of the ball, which was now rolling in the opposite direction; he ran over to grab it. The two of them sat down on the mat and tossed the ball back and forth. Every time Moshe threw the ball, Dan was forced to get up and chase after it, while the little boy giggled with joy. His black eyes doubled in size from happiness over the attention Dan was giving him.

Leah stood back and enjoyed the heartwarming sight.

Finally, Dan glanced at his watch. "I have to go," he said, partly to Moshe and partly to himself.

Before he left, Leah said to him, "Nothing we tried, not candy or dolls or anything else, could get a smile out of that girl. It was only because of you that I saw her smile. Thank you."

Chapter 4

During recess, after I had gone a few days of rarely seeing Dan in private (because he went everywhere with *her*), he turned to me and said, "Michal . . . come here for a second." I rushed over to him and thought, *Maybe. . . .*

"Michal," he said, repeating my name. His eyes deep and piercing, he asked, "Could you let Miriam in on your game too?"

I was furious. I didn't want to, but I was worried about losing Dan and my position in class; I was class queen and he was the king. I couldn't give up his blue eyes, and this was an opportunity to renew our bond. And so I pulled Miriam after me.

We brought her into our game of "Rag Tag,"[5] and made room for her in the circle. It was my turn to drop the rag behind one of the girls sitting in the circle. I dropped it behind Abigail. She immediately leapt up and dropped the rag behind Yael, who dropped the rag behind Miriam. Rina, who saw the rag behind Miriam, tried to explain the game to her with hand gestures. Miriam got up, and instead of running after Yael, she dropped the rag behind my back and held her spot. I jumped up and tried to catch her. She ran. I took after her, fueled by hate as much as the goal of the game. Eventually, she stopped running and I caught her.

We sat her down in the middle of the circle, and we all sang the Rag Tag Song. We weren't mocking her—this was part of the game. But there was ridicule hidden in our voices. Miriam didn't understand the game. When

---

5   "Rag Tag" was a variation of the game "Duck, Duck, Goose." The participants sit in a circle, and one of the players gets up and walks behind the others, holding an object—commonly a rag. The player outside the circle drops the rag behind the back of a second player in the circle and tries to run back to his original spot. The second player, who had the rag dropped behind him, must catch the first player before he can reach his spot. If the first player makes it back to his place in the circle before getting caught, the second player is now left outside the circle to drop the rag behind someone else, while the other players sing "The Rag Tag Song" at him.

she sat there, stuck in the middle like that with all of us singing at her, she must have felt embarrassed—like she was under attack. Overwhelmed, she shot up and ran off to the toddlers' room. No one went after her.

When she walked in, the small boy with a head of black curls ran up to her. She hugged him and said, in Polish, "Why did we come here? Are you happy? Or do you feel like I do?" She clutched him to her chest with all her might. Seeing his sister crying miserably, he stroked her hair and kissed her.

The kindergarten children stared at them, but it didn't bother her. Miriam had mixed feelings about the toddlers. She loved them all for taking her brother in without scorn, but she feared them, too, worrying that they might steal him away from her and leave her all alone. She was afraid he would grow up to become a child of the kibbutz—one of them, fundamentally different from her.

The bell rang for the students to head to their classes, but Miriam, as if deaf to it, remained there, hugging her brother. "They won't take me away from here," she said in Polish, emotionally. "Never!"

All the children of the kibbutz went to their classrooms, and so did I. When I walked in, I saw Dan. I was angry with him and wanted to make him jealous. So, I went over to him and said that because Esther was sick, and her seat was in the middle of the classroom, I'd take her spot, which "just happened" to be next to Joel.

Dan wasn't angry. All he said was, "Okay, if that's what you want. But come back—we are friends after all."

"Friends," I laughed bitterly to myself. "Real friends . . ."

The class went much differently than I had expected. Dan didn't look at me or at the empty chair by his side. He kept his eyes on the door, occasionally looking out the window. The only time he did otherwise was when the teacher called on him. He glanced at me for a moment, without much affection, then over at Abigail and Yael, and then he raised his hand. The teacher called his name and asked what he wanted.

"May I be excused for a minute?" he asked.

She allowed it. "Maybe it'll help him concentrate," she mumbled under her breath.

Dan left the room, and I watched him through the window. He turned toward the houses before moving out of sight.

Dan ran over to the toddlers' room. From the doorway, he saw Miriam on the floor with her back to him. She and her brother had built an odd little house. Inside they'd placed a small wooden plank, and on it were four dolls. Dan lightly caressed her hair to make his presence known. She turned sharply and let out a sigh of relief, seeing it was him standing behind her. She smiled at him, and he returned the smile. Dan wanted to befriend her, so he joined their game of blocks. But she wouldn't let him. Why, he didn't know. She sensed his fierce desire to join in and tried to explain herself. "Ghetto,"[6] she said, and pointed at the odd-looking building made out of blocks. When he still did not understand, she used what little Hebrew she knew to say, "No . . . you . . . house." He understood her words, but still couldn't quite grasp what she was trying to tell him—that she had built a ghetto.

He tried to take her to class, but she wouldn't budge no matter how hard he tried to convince her. Finally, after what seemed like an hour, she was willing to part with her little brother and go back to class—although

---

6   During World War II, when the Nazis would take over a city in Europe, they would force all Jews in that city into a small neighborhood. These neighborhoods were called ghettos, and they were known for their horrible living conditions, which included severe overcrowding, terrible hunger, dangerously poor hygiene and filth, abuse, and a lack of basic necessities. Ghettos were fenced in and heavily guarded by Nazi soldiers so that its inhabitants could not escape. Many Jewish people were killed in the ghettos; for those who survived them, they were merely the first stop on the way to the death camps.

Dan still wasn't sure just what had changed her mind. Before they left, Dan also asked her to take apart the odd building-block ghetto. But she refused and protected it with her arms when he tried to help.

As they headed for the classroom, an idea came to Dan. He picked up a stone from the main path, turned to Miriam and said, "Stone." He repeated the word a few times, until Miriam picked up a stone of her own and said, "Stone."

Then, a mischievous glint came to his eye. He raised his hand, and with a sudden snap he threw the stone into the toddlers' room, aiming it at the building-block house. Seeing the stone roll away in a different direction, he shrugged. Miriam smiled awkwardly, as if to say, *The ghetto is stronger than us.*

They kept walking along the path to the classroom while Dan tried teaching her more words, and then a complete sentence in Hebrew: "I want to sit down and study."

He knocked on the classroom door. "Yes?" said the teacher. The two of them walked in and faced the class. Dan gestured to Miriam, and she said, "Teach-er, I want sit down and stu-dy."

"Very nice," said the teacher. The rest of us chuckled, enjoying ourselves. "But say, *to* sit down."

"*To* sit down," Miriam repeated happily after the teacher.

"Excellent." The teacher smiled at them, and scanned the classroom for an open seat. "Ah," she said. "You can sit next to Dan, and he'll help you with your schoolwork. And also . . ." The teacher blushed, and quickly resumed her lesson. I was so angry with her for doing this.

Miriam was truly proud of the new words she learned every day, and she rehearsed them over and over. During recess one day, Miriam sat alone mumbling words to herself. She resolved to make more of an effort in her schoolwork from now on. She sat down on a rock and began to make plans.

She was so lost in thought that when I walked by and stuck out my tongue at her, it was like I didn't exist. Just then, the teacher called the students back to class. Miriam took her seat and tried to listen, but it was all so different from the daydream she'd spun for herself during recess. In the dream, the new language was clear and comprehensible, whereas now it seemed dense and dark. The teacher's words, those odd syllables in that funny-sounding language, whizzed right by her ears until, once again, she found herself staring out the window.

She wasn't the only one. Everyone was either dozing off or doodling on their papers, while the teacher droned on and on about how to solve a certain math problem.

The teacher, who'd finally paused to take a quick breath, noticed this widespread inattention and said, "Well, I've lectured you all for . . ." she glanced at her watch . . . "about half an hour. Now that everything is clear, I'm sure you won't mind being quizzed on it."

Everybody sat up in their seats.

"Quiz . . . quiz!" The word rippled through the class.

The teacher continued calmly, "Yes, I'm sure you can all be quizzed on it. The quiz will be very simple. Everybody take out a sheet of paper, please."

"Teacher, don't you think that would be a waste of paper?" said one student, while another tried, "We worked hard in the barn all day." But it was no use. The teacher would not give in.

We didn't like her. Usually we had classes with our homeroom teacher, but for math, "Wicked Rivka" would come over from the neighboring kibbutz and torture us with all kinds of dirty teachers' tricks—like this quiz.

"Hurry up." The teacher raised her voice. "I haven't got all day. Take out your papers and pens." She wrote an odd math problem on the blackboard, and we copied it down and tried to solve it.

Everybody whispered, "Do you know anything?"

"Do you?"

"I have no idea."

"Quiet!" Wicked Rivka said loudly.

We all fell silent. Everybody sat there, staring back and forth from the teacher to the blank page.

Just one girl in the back of the class worked hard at the problem—the same girl I hated so deeply. She knew how to solve it. The children who sat on either side of Miriam sucked up to her and asked her to explain the solution. What an outrage! Sucking up for some silly quiz! But deep inside, I thought to myself, *You have to solve this problem. You just have to.* But it was no use. The answer to this horrible math problem refused to pop into my head. Miriam walked up to the teacher first and handed in her quiz. Then she walked back to her seat and prayed that her answer was correct.

"All pages up front." Wicked Rivka raised her mean voice. She seemed pleased with the first quiz that had been handed in. The rest of us were forced to hand over blank pieces of paper. Even Dan, who had earned the nickname "The Good Boy" ever since he befriended Miriam, failed the quiz.

After all the quizzes had been collected, the teacher began to scold us. "There are fourteen of you here in this class," she said.

"Thirteen," a student quickly corrected her.

"Thirteen of you here in this class," she said. "And only one girl solved the problem correctly. This tells me that you kids are simply not listening!"

Rivka's boring speech nearly put me to sleep. And then she said, "I'll repeat the lesson one more time, and then you'll be quizzed on it again. Any student who fails the second quiz . . ." She stopped there, but everyone knew exactly what she meant and listened closely.

"Miriam, come," said the teacher. "Solve the problem on the blackboard for us." Miriam didn't understand what the teacher was saying, so Dan pointed toward the blackboard and tried to explain what the teacher wanted her to do. She got up, hesitant at first, and then quickly solved the complicated problem on the board. When she was done, she returned to her seat. Dan looked at her with admiration. "We'll continue this tomorrow," said Wicked Rivka, just as we were saved by the bell.

During recess, the students huddled together in groups and complained. One boy grumbled, "That teacher and all those grown-ups . . . they always like the new ones better than they like us. They're nicer to the ones who come from over there." We all stared at Miriam.

Chapter 5

The kibbutz had been humming since morning; everyone was hard at work. The dining room was tidied and decorated. We were expecting newcomers yet again. Amar and Saul, Dan and Yael's fathers, mowed the big lawn, while my mother and Abigail's mother fixed up the rooms for another group of incoming immigrants.

Everybody had a task. Leah slaved away in the barn, though she was no expert at milking, to make sure the newcomers had fresh milk. Rachel and Dvora left the washroom sparkling clean, and moved on to the chicken coop, where they got two chickens and a basket overflowing with eggs. That evening, we would have a royal feast.

Time sped by, and by noon all the kibbutz members were anxiously standing by the side of the road. Waiting. Silently praying for a miracle.

Our excitement mounted as we saw the bus appear

in the distance. I looked at my mother. She was excited. So was Leah. Everybody waited, holding their breath in anticipation. Maybe here, on this bus, they'd find their lost relatives.[7] The outdated bus crawled its way toward us and stopped in the main square, raising a cloud of dust around it. People started coughing, and clothes were unwittingly stained, but no one cared.

The bus opened its doors, and a group of people stepped out. All were dragging tattered suitcases and bundles of cloth, with blankets tied around their belongings. Most of the men were unshaven. Their eyes were sunken and tired, especially the gaunt elderly men and women, who leaned on the younger ones for support. Some were clearly excited, while others were still shocked and overwhelmed. Saul encouraged them with cries of "Welcome!" Even we, the children, were waiting for them. We had no idea who they were, but we waited just like the adults.

7　　During the Holocaust, Jewish people were often separated from their family members due to circumstances beyond their control. Arrest by the Nazis, violence and harassment, escape, and being sent to concentration camps (where males and females were held separately) resulted in many loved ones losing contact with one another. When the war ended, people struggled to find out what had happened to their families or friends. Some organizations were put together to help, but it was difficult. A few people were lucky and found someone they had lost; many others were not.

Miriam stood by Leah, holding her hand, and looked on with hope in her eyes. Who was she waiting for? Suddenly, Leah let go of her hand and ran up to one of the newcomers. He was surprised to see her running toward him, as were we. But we smiled. At least one kibbutz member had found her family. They fell into each other's arms and stayed that way for a few moments. When they let go, Leah whispered lovingly, "Uncle Yankel!"

"Henya!" he replied.

At that, they fell silent. They realized they had made a mistake.

"I'm sorry," Leah apologized. "I thought you were . . ."

"Me, too. I thought you were someone else."

Another hope shattered; Leah wiped a single tear off her cheek. We had seen it before, yet we knew they would never stop hoping, praying they'd see their loved ones again.

The other immigrants stepped off the bus and eventually made their way into the kibbutz, toward the rooms, accompanied by the members. The main square was now empty. Only a few remnants—a bench or two, flags, a table, a pitcher of cold water and glasses of orange juice— told of the joy and excitement that had just taken place there.

Just Leah and that man stayed behind. Leah apologized over and over for her mistake. He took off his hat, revealing his white, mostly bald head. "Sit down, my child," he requested. She sat down on the bench by his side. "What is your name?" he asked.

"Leah," she replied. "And yours?"

"Manek. You know, I had a niece like you once. Her name was Henya. Her hair was the color of yours, and her eyes were the color of yours."

"And I . . . I thought you were my uncle Yankel," she said sadly. "His walk was like your walk, and his smile was like your smile."

The two of them fell silent. Then, Leah perked up. "I almost forgot," she said, pointing to the pitcher of water. "Would you like something to drink?"

"Yes, I'd like a glass of fresh milk very much," he said.

"Wait right here," she said, and ran to the kitchen, just as she had as a child, when she'd run to fetch whatever her father asked for. And, in fact, she felt like a child again. She tilted the giant container so that fresh, white milk flowed into the glass in her hand. The milk filled the cup and overflowed, spilling everywhere. Leah smiled to herself. Bracha, who was passing by and noticed this, was displeased. Spilling was wasteful.

"Leah? Are you alright?" she asked, a hint of reproach in her voice.

Distracted, Leah didn't answer as she left with the glass of milk. She came back to the main square and saw Manek looking around and taking in his new surroundings. She was about to sit down by his side when Yael came running up, out of breath.

"Leah, come quickly!" she panted. "We were playing in the field, and Dan fell down. He's bleeding . . . from his head."

In her panic, Leah dropped the glass of milk. She urged Yael, "Run off and get the nurse!" She herself ran toward the field where the children were playing. She'd been so preoccupied with Manek that she'd forgotten to watch over them.

She came running. Dan was still lying there in the center of a makeshift soccer court, the sand lot the children used as a playing field. "Dan," she whispered, leaning over him.

Immediately following Leah was the nurse with her first aid kit, who bandaged Dan's head. Dan rose to his feet, leaning on Leah and the nurse.

We walked him to the room. Everybody sat around his bed. Leah sat by my side and held Dan's hand.

Dan's mother was there too; she'd heard the news and dropped everything to come and sit by his side, caressing his brown hair. There was a sudden knock on the door, and Manek—the man from the bus—walked in. All eyes turned to him. He had a kind smile, like a grandfather.

"Hello there, young man," he said to Dan.

Dan didn't answer; he just nodded hello.

Leah welcomed Manek and said, "Come in, have a seat." She gave him her spot and sat with the children.

"How do you feel?" asked Manek. Dan smiled. "Did you hit your head? Don't worry, it'll pass."

The room was quiet. Manek looked around. Preparations for Hanukkah[8] were underway, and paper decorations, menorahs fashioned out of different objects, and candles and dreidels[9] were left on the floor from a recent game. He picked up one of the dreidels and studied it. After a few moments of silence, he looked up at us

---

8   Hanukkah: A Jewish holiday lasting eight days that commemorates the victory of the Maccabean Revolt, the rededication of the Temple, and the miracle of the jug of oil. The holiday is celebrated with prayers of thanks and praise, and a ceremonial lighting of the Hanukkah candles on each night of the festival.

9   A dreidel is a children's toy, a spinning top with four sides. In Jewish culture, the dreidel is a traditional Hanukkah game.

and said, "Would you like me to tell you a story about a real Hanukkah miracle?"

Dan nodded, as did the rest of us. And Manek began his story:

"I'm sure you know there was a war with the German Nazis. Thank the Lord, the war ended, and here I am, in the land of Israel." He shook his head in disbelief, still amazed that he'd actually made it. "Well, it seemed nearly certain that the Nazis could and would kill all the Jews and leave not a trace of us. Before the war, I lived in a large, fancy house with my wife, my son, and my sister and her daughter. By the time we felt we were in danger, it was already too late to flee the country. So, we stayed where we lived, until we heard what the Nazis had done in the neighboring town and decided we should try to get away. Along with our neighbors, we found a small hiding place where we stashed all our belongings.

"Some believed it was an excellent hiding place for people, as well as their belongings, and they decided to hide there. Most of our neighbors did this, and my sister decided it was best for her to stay as well, since the danger of being on the road seemed far greater.

"We said our goodbyes to everybody, and we wandered

for days upon nights. My wife resembled an Aryan,[10] so she did not need to hide. She'd hand-roll cigarettes and sell them to people for spare change, which she'd use to buy us food as best she could. I, on the other hand, a Jew in both appearance and temperament"—he chuckled as he said these words—"I hid with my little boy and waited for her return. One day, she never came back. I looked for her everywhere. After a few days, I gave up. I understood that I would never see her again. . . ." Manek spoke softly, practically whispering those last few words. Then, he pulled a white handkerchief from his pocket and used it to dab at his wet eyes. We averted our gaze, and Manek continued:

"We were forced, my son and I, to leave our hiding place and wander through various towns, looking for food and shelter. One day, as I walked through one of these towns, I knocked fearfully on the door of a house at the side of the road. To my surprise, the woman who opened the door was related to my wife. I knew she lived

---

10   The Nazis believed that the "Aryans" were a race of people who were superior to all others. They characterized Aryans as people with fair skin, blond hair, pale eyes, and longer, oval-shaped faces. The Nazis wanted to get rid of non-Aryan people—like Jews, Gypsies, and other minority groups—so that Aryans could fulfill their "duty" (as the Nazis saw it) of controlling the world.

somewhere near there, but I didn't know exactly where. I was overjoyed to finally see a friendly face. She took us into her house and fed us delicacies we hadn't tasted in a very long time.

"I told her everything we'd been through in great detail. She told me there was a man in the neighboring town who could forge documents that might help us escape. Somewhat apprehensively, she wrote his address down for me on a piece of paper. I decided to try my luck and get documents for the both of us. In the meantime, to avoid putting my son in danger, I asked if I could leave him with her until I returned.

"She agreed, and I left, following her directions to the address she'd given me. The distance was roughly twenty-five kilometers,[11] and I had no choice but to make the journey on foot. It took a lot of effort and money, but eventually I got the documents. A few days had passed by the time I completed my mission and returned to town. But by then, the town was no longer there."

Manek's voice was different now, deeper and drenched in sadness.

"It was a desolate dump. The relatives and my boy

---

11   Twenty-five kilometers is fifteen and a half miles.

were no longer there. I searched for days. I asked people what had happened there and heard their stories. I knew it was a lost cause. So, I continued on my journey alone. It went on that way for many months.

"Throughout the entire war I fought hard to save my life. What kept me going was a vow I made for myself, to one day go to the land of Israel and tell the world what had happened to us, in memory of my wife and child. And when the war was over, when the allies finally defeated the Germans, I felt alone in this world, and I decided to go back to my town to find any surviving relatives. When I got there, I found nothing at all. The looters had taken everything. No one was left, an entire Jewish community evaporated, and all our family belongings, too. Not even a photograph, a tiny charm, or a piece of clothing was left behind for me to keep as a precious souvenir. I dug up the spot where we'd buried our belongings, but I found nothing except for a piece of paper with the words 'Mama, Manek was right!' written in a child's handwriting. When I read the words, I could hear the voices that might have written or said them. I didn't know if one of the neighbors' children had written it or if it was my sister's daughter. But I understood how terribly they had suffered."

He pulled a torn piece of paper from his pocket, folded

and wrapped in plastic, and showed it to the children. We gazed at the page in wonder. Manek continued:

"I gave up hope of finding any trace of my family, so I made do with this precious piece of paper. I went to a tavern. Pioter, the Polish bartender, was still there, pouring beer just like he had in the days before the war. I took a seat at the bar. Pioter turned to me and asked, astonished, 'Manek?!' 'Yes,' I responded.

"He hugged me warmly. 'Manek, my friend,' he said. 'I saw them . . . I saw how they took them away.'

"I asked him countless questions, to learn everything I could about the fate of my family. Pioter told me everything he knew and what he had heard from others. I listened closely.

"I wanted to know everything about them. Maybe there was still a chance of finding them? But he kept cutting his story short because he had to serve someone a drink or because someone asked him a question. I looked around. Everything was exactly the same. Nothing had changed. But then I remembered that before the war Pioter had a painting hanging of a flowing river. My wife had loved that painting. I looked around for it. I wanted to etch it into my memory, maybe even buy it. But in its place on the wall, there was . . ."

At this point, Manek stopped telling his story. We all stared at him, waiting, curious. We thirsted for his words. What happened next? Then, he continued:

"Hanging on the wall, I saw a menorah. It wasn't too big, and it was made of copper. Pioter saw the shock on my face and said, 'Oh, that. One day some merchant came by and sold it to me. To be honest with you, I don't even know what the thing is used for.' He said this dismissively.

"'Will you sell it to me?' I asked and pulled out all the coins in my possession.

"Pioter looked at all my money and said, 'That's too much, my friend. I'll sell it to you for 100 zlotys.'"[12] Manek chuckled and explained, "That, too, is a lot of money. He took the menorah down off the wall and handed it to me. That menorah was dear to my heart and is still precious to me. I got it from my father-in-law, who got it from his father-in-law. Imagine my joy at finding that precious treasure." Manek untied his bundle of clothes and revealed the menorah hidden deep inside. He showed it to us and said:

"I stayed in Poland for a while, and then I decided to finally come to the land of Israel. But there was one problem. The authorities didn't allow us to take our personal

---

12   100 zlotys (Polish currency) is equal to 25 dollars.

possessions with us—nothing but clothes and essentials. So, I baked a big loaf of bread, hid the menorah inside it and got ready to leave the country. When I reached the port, where they checked our luggage to see if we'd followed their strict orders, the officers noticed my big loaf of bread. 'What is that?' an officer asked. 'It's food,' I told him. 'We have a long journey ahead of us, and I might get hungry.'

"He nodded suspiciously. I'm not sure he believed me, but eventually he let me through. I breathed a sigh of relief that I was able to fool him and reach the land of Israel with the menorah . . . to tell you this story."

Manek finished his story, and we were left with tears in our eyes, unable to move or say a word.

Suddenly, Dan's mother said, "Children, what do you think about staging Manek's story as our Hanukkah play?" She turned to him and said, "I'm sorry. Only if you agree to it first, of course."

"It would be a great honor," he said, and then added, "I love children, but I have no one left in the world. Will you accept me as your uncle?"

"Yes, Uncle Manek!" we all cried out.

Leah stood up. "And now, children, to the dining hall. We've got a celebration dinner to go to. Let's let Dan rest."

Chapter 6

The Hanukkah party was getting closer and closer. As time passed, I grew more and more concerned, because the play was based on Manek's story, and Miriam, who'd come from over there—and by now was, to my amazement, speaking Hebrew well but with a heavy accent—was given one of the best parts: Manek's wife. The role of Manek, of course, was promised to Dan.

At mealtime, my worries were interrupted by Rina, Yael's mother, who was the show coordinator in addition to being in charge of laundry for the kibbutz, as she walked into the dining hall. "Quiet, children, quiet down," she said as she tried to silence the ruckus around our table. "I have an announcement for you," she said. "Today we'll be having a rehearsal. While we're there, we'll have a chance to decide if the children we picked last week will still be playing the parts chosen for them.

Anyone who doesn't show up for rehearsal will not be in the play. Michal." The teacher turned to me. "Come see me after the meal."

I finished eating and walked over to the teacher's table. "Michal," she said quietly. "Miriam and Dan are on duty right now. Please let them know about the meeting at four o'clock."

"Sure, of course," I said.

I stepped out of the dining hall. To my delight, Miriam just happened to pass by.

"Today, at six, there's a rehearsal for the play," I told her confidently.

"Isn't that late?" she asked in wonder.

"I don't know. That's what I was told," I said, and ran off to look for Dan. I found him in the chicken coop. I didn't linger there; I gave him the message, word for word, and went off to work in the barn.

Night fell, and the hour of the rehearsal came and went.

Yael's mom made good on her threat, and when Miriam failed to show up, she cancelled her participation in the play. The role of Manek's wife fell to me.

At exactly six o'clock, out on the lawn, away from everybody else, a girl stood waiting, tapping her little feet.

After waiting a long time, she finally gave up, and she went off to the toddlers' room. When she walked in, the caretaker greeted her by whispering, "Hush . . . hush. They just fell asleep." But Miriam nevertheless pushed the door open and stormed in. The babies sleeping peacefully filled her with a warm and pleasant feeling. She walked over to her brother's bed. He still slept restlessly, and would wake up several times a night, frightened and yelling words Miriam could not understand, before falling back asleep. She looked at him with sorrow and love. Their mother would have been proud if she could see them now, she thought. "Mama," he mumbled, as if reading her mind, and at that moment she missed their mom with all her heart. By his bed, Miriam left him a piece of chocolate that she'd gotten and saved for him all day. From there, she went to the children's communal room. Everybody was at the dining room at the time.

She opened the dresser by her bed, which was nothing but a wooden box with a drawer in it, and pulled out her old dress, the one she'd worn when she arrived in Israel. She'd kept it as a souvenir. Miriam held it in her hand. The dress seemed so different to her now, and it smelled bad.

Have I adapted to the kibbutz? she wondered. She looked

at her clothes. They were identical to the clothes of all the other children on the kibbutz—a short-sleeved shirt and pants which revealed skinny little legs. Suddenly, she noticed me, standing at the doorway watching her. We looked at each other. And then she averted her eyes. Meanwhile, my eyes sparkled and remained fixed on her. She got up from her bed and turned to leave.

I felt a pang of sadness at the pitiful sight. I'd never felt that way before. Was I changing?

She stopped before leaving and stared at me, her gaze piercing. Then she left the room, walking slowly. I moved toward the exit and kept watching her. Rina, who was strolling along the path, walked over to her. "Are you going to get some food?" she asked.

"Yes," Miriam answered, sounding angry.

"Are you in a bad mood or what?" asked Rina.

"No, it's nothing," Miriam said dismissively, before walking even faster.

"Why didn't you come to the rehearsal?" asked Rina, who matched her steps to Miriam's.

"*I* didn't come?!" Miriam exclaimed in wonder. "I waited for you for half an hour."

"When did you come?" asked Rina.

"At six."

"Well, of course. You could have waited for us until tomorrow and it wouldn't have done any good. The rehearsal was at four."

"At four? But Michal told me that . . ."

"I don't understand. Let's discuss this tomorrow and sort it out," Rina said.

"Thanks," Miriam said.

But Miriam did not run off to the dining room. Instead, she turned back to the children's room.

I was still standing at the doorway. She asked me, "Are you going to eat?"

"In a little bit," I answered.

"Can I join you?" she asked.

"What do you want?" I asked, firmly.

"Just to talk. You are the class queen, after all. Who better to talk to than the queen?"

I could tell what she wanted from her tone and the look in her eye. And, to be honest, my conscience was weighing on me.

"You . . . want . . . to know why I told you the rehearsal was at six?" I asked.

"Only if you want to tell me; I won't force you," she replied.

I looked at her again. She was a girl just like me, the

same age as me, wearing the same clothes as me. What was I doing to her? I pondered this. And I decided to tell her. I built up the courage, and without forgetting my status as class queen, I said, "Because—"

"It doesn't matter," Miriam cut me off good-naturedly and spared me the embarrassment of answering. "Friends?" she asked and put her hand on my shoulder. It was as if she understood me, and I was unprepared for her forgiveness.

I moved my arm quickly, pushing her hand off my shoulder. I glared at her as if to say, *Who do you think you are, touching me?!*

She said nothing more, but shuffled toward the door and stopped there. I expected her to burst into tears, to curse at me, to stare at me with hatred in her eyes. But she just shot a quick, arrogant glance back at me, and then ran off to the dining hall.

I stood frozen in the doorway, ashamed of myself. I wanted to run after her and apologize, but I quickly changed my mind. Why should *I* chase after *her*?!

Rina walked by and stopped. "I didn't see you in the dining hall. Where are you headed?" she asked.

"To the barn," I said. "I'm still on duty."

"And what about getting something to eat?" Since I

shrugged with disinterest, she added, "What's troubling you, Michal?"

"I . . ." I tried to answer her.

She said nothing, but stood there, fascinated.

"I . . . said . . ." I was able to add one more word to my previous sentence. But my voice was once again unsure of itself. Was this the right move?

"I . . . I told Miriam to come to the rehearsal at . . ." I stopped and hesitated. I gazed at the ground and at my shoes. They needed mending, I thought to myself, as if trying to distract myself. But Rina wouldn't give up, and she urged me to keep talking. At last, the words came out of my mouth. "I told her to come to the rehearsal at six instead of four."

"Well, then," Rina said. "This means she'll be getting her part back, and I think you should apologize to her." She spoke firmly. I averted my eyes again. My shoes really did need mending. "Go get something to eat; you're looking a little pale," she added softly.

"Yes," I said. "And . . . thank you."

"Thank you, too," Rina whispered to me.

I ran toward the dining hall through all the buildings. I wanted to disappear as quickly as I could from Rina's gaze, which kept following me and torturing me. And still, I felt relief. I could think more clearly.

The Hanukkah party, which I'd looked forward to for so long and had such high hopes for was, eventually, a disappointment. Not because it wasn't joyous, and not because the food wasn't good, but because she was there—on stage, with her skinny body, playing the lead part, while I made do with a background part. It spoiled my holiday cheer.

She played her part so beautifully that all the kibbutz members, new and old, were moved to tears by the story.

I stared at the audience. Manek seemed odd, staring sharply at the stage. His eyes pierced her so deeply—as if he were trying to uncover her soul—and then filled up with love as he watched her move lightly and delicately across the stage. It was clear—she really did remind him of his wife.

When the show was over, the members milled about the decorated dining hall, among tables set with all kinds of food: Hanukkah donuts, potato pancakes, and other special holiday treats that we never had on regular days. Manek walked over to Miriam, who was still buzzing

with excitement from the play, and said, "You acted so well; it was so real."

"Thank you," she replied.

"Your movements were so graceful, I thought for a moment I was looking at my dear wife."

"Were you in Poland too?" she asked.

"Yes, with my wife and my child, and we suffered like all the Jews."

Just then, David, the secretary of the kibbutz, interrupted and said, "Manek, we need you at the main office."

"Thank you, Miriam," Manek said again.

"Thank you, Uncle Manek," she answered.

As he left, Manek headed toward the kibbutz's main office without turning back for fear that she would notice the tears in his eyes.

Chapter 7

That miserable night of the Hanukkah party would have stayed with me for days if our kibbutz hadn't received waves of illegal immigrants smuggled in from Europe. They braved a treacherous journey to reach us. Most were penniless, without possessions or family. The sight of them was gut-wrenching.

The order of the day was to be one great big family.

In the evenings we gathered around them and listened intently to their horrifying stories of life in the ghettos, the extermination camps, and the forests. So sad were their tales that even the children cried, alongside their equally disheartened parents. Later, when we went back to our rooms, the adults muttered to themselves, "How? How could this happen?"

Among the immigrants was Samuel, a skinny man who

must have been in his thirties, though he looked much older. After spending several days with us without uttering a word, the members finally urged him to talk. As he did, his story was so horrific that they asked us children to leave the dining hall.

Samuel sobbed bitter tears. He spoke of his children; he'd had two—a seven-year-old son and a four-year-old daughter. The three of them were sent to a death camp, and. . . .

That was all we, the children, were allowed to hear.

The morning after Samuel told his story, Dan seemed exceptionally troubled. Right after the teacher dismissed us for recess, he ran toward the houses and stopped there. I walked after him, but he didn't notice me. He sat under a tree facing Leah's room and mumbled something to himself that sounded like, "She asked me to stop, said it was nothing. She said that she was just moved by Samuel's story. But I know that's not true . . . something happened to her yesterday, to Leah."

Dan looked over at the small shed. Its door opened slowly. Leah was about to step out, but when she noticed us, or rather him, she disappeared swiftly back into the shed and shut herself inside her house. I hid behind the olive tree. Dan got up and approached the house. He was about to knock on the door, but before he had the chance, it opened.

Now I worried that Leah had locked herself in her room because of me. I came near the small shed and strained to hear what was said on the other side of the door. I knew it was wrong of me to eavesdrop, but I was mesmerized; I had to find out what was going on. Curiosity consumed me. I had to find out why they were having this mysterious meeting. Standing there, I looked to both sides, then put my ear up to the door. I heard fragments like "Smuggling . . ." "Underground . . ." and "What do you know?" These snippets only fanned the flames of my curiosity.

I knocked hesitantly.

Leah opened up for me, and I immediately noticed the storm in her eyes. She slid her hand down my hair. "Come in," she said, and sat me down on the little box in her room, which was small with white walls decorated with Leah's paintings. Other than the box I sat on, there were a couple of painted wooden boxes she used for chairs and a small wooden table. Another small table stood out in the room, placed to the side of the metal

bed. It was a round table covered with a handkerchief tablecloth, white with embroidered flowers. On the table there stood a framed photograph of a four-year-old girl.

Leah had tears in her eyes, and she knew I could see them. She picked up the picture of the girl from the table (I could see her hands had a mild tremor) and tried to explain.

"I don't know why, but with the illegal immigrants coming to our kibbutz day in and day out, telling their stories and bearing their souls, it's getting harder for me to keep my secret any longer. I've been so ashamed of it." She fell silent, and then added, "I don't know why I invited you, of all people, Dan. After you saw me crying the other day, while we listened to Samuel's story, when he arrived at the kibbutz . . . they say children know how to listen. Yesterday I thought I'd have the strength to tell my story, but today . . . I'm not sure I can do it."

Leah was quiet for a while, and so were we. She stared at us, as if about to come to a decision, and then abruptly started speaking. "I'll try . . . I'll try to tell you something I've never told anyone before." She said that, and once again went quiet. After a while, she broke her long silence with the words: "I lied to you! I didn't come to Israel as a little girl; I came as a young woman, when I was twenty-two years old. All my friends came here from Europe by dangerous means, before the war, because they predicted the coming danger. They asked me to join them, to lay the groundwork for the arrival of other groups of illegal immigrants." Leah's breathing was erratic, and after a long pause, she whispered, "Most of them never got to see our homeland."

"I remember my best friend's words: 'Come, darling, come to the Holy Land, to plow and harvest, to raise your little Mary . . . come . . . come . . .'" Leah whispered, as if talking to herself. "And I really did want to go with them. The treacherous path, the dangers, they scared us all, but I wanted it so badly," Leah said, choking on her tears. "That day, I was going to refuse my friend's offer." She spoke to the window. "Children were not allowed on the smuggling boats and having Mary aboard would have endangered the entire group. And I loved my Mary too much to leave without her. My Mary . . . the last thing I had left from Josef, the love of my life."

Leah quickly sketched the figure of a man on a sheet of paper tossed on the table. His hair was short, and his eyes were big and full of life. "Josef," she mumbled. "Fate . . . took them away. . . ." she added with anger, looking upward.

Dan and I were alarmed by her odd behavior and rambling sentences.

"In those days, after his death," Leah tried to bravely keep going. "I was hurt, I was hateful, I was scared. . . ."

"Leah," we whispered to her. "This isn't doing you any good, telling us all this. Please, stop."

I tried to hug her, but she pushed me away.

"Let me get it off my chest," she begged us. "There is so much I've been trying to hide all this time." She continued: "I held out hope, but now I know. None of them made it out alive." She sat back down. "My good friend Sylvia offered to take care of my Mary because it was too dangerous to bring a child with me. We agreed they would join us in the land of Israel later, after I was settled.

"I wish . . . I wish I'd never made it. I wish they'd made it instead of me, or at least my brother Jacob, who died in my arms on the way here. I still remember his last words. He whispered: 'The homeland. How much I wanted to see it! But you, Leah, you will see it for me.' And he smiled," Leah cried out. "How could he have smiled like that, at his moment of death? Did my mother and father smile when they were taken to the death camps? And my Mary? Did she smile too?"

Leah burst into tears. Dan and I shook her. "Calm down," Dan pleaded. "All this is in the past; you shouldn't do this to yourself."

"Dan!" She raised her voice. "Will I ever be able to stop the tears? Will I be able to forget the pain of giving my child away? Yes. Yes. I gave her to Sylvia because I was afraid of the danger ahead of me. I wanted to protect her. And now Sylvia, along with her own children and my Mary, are gone. How could I leave her, abandon my daughter—my own flesh and blood—and delude myself into thinking they'd arrive after me?" Leah's shrieks terrified us, but she would not stop, no matter how much we implored her.

Leah eventually calmed down and got her story in order.

"I wanted to come to Israel and pave the way for my family and for others, but I was so afraid of giving Mary away. And yet, when the day came for me to give her to Sylvia, I still did it. I took her to Sylvia's house, and it seemed so grand and safe there. The rooms were all so big and spacious, stylish and full of beautiful furniture. Sylvia was beautiful too; in her long, embroidered dress she looked just like a princess. She always wore a gold ring studded with a beautiful red ruby stone on her finger. She smiled at me, graceful and confident, and said, 'Go, darling, make your dream—*our* dream—come true. And when you're ready . . . I will . . . I will come to Israel with your daughter.' Sylvia's voice broke as she said this. And I . . ." Leah cried out. "I didn't understand why she hesitated that way. But she knew! Then she said, 'I promise I'll guard her with my life; I'd give everything I own to keep your daughter safe. You can be sure of that.' *Everything I own*," Leah cried. "All that property of theirs—those beautiful things—it was why Sylvia stayed behind for so long. They waited just one more day and one more day, until it was too late. And now, because of all that property, Sylvia and my daughter are not with me today."

Leah tried to calm down. Dan and I looked at each other, stunned by the story Leah had kept locked in her heart all these years. I couldn't even believe my own ears, and my mind was racing in disbelief. Leah had had a child; she could have been our age. A few minutes passed before Leah picked up where she had left off:

"The man who'd married Sylvia was handsome and strong. He had fair hair and eyes as blue as yours," she said, turning to Dan and looking deep into his eyes. She was speaking in a softer voice now. "They invited me to their holiday dinner before my trip. I walked into their house with Mary in my arms. Sylvia wanted to take her off my hands, but I refused. We sat down at the table, me, my Mary, Sylvia, her husband, and their little daughter, who was dressed in all white, and was so excited to hear that Mary would be staying with them. And I thought: *How could war possibly come to such a peaceful place? What if the group and I are leaving for nothing? After all, we might not even make it to Israel. Here, in Poland, everything is so pleasant and beautiful, while our journey to Israel will bring nothing but danger.* I almost changed my mind. I think I would have, had I known what was going to happen to them," she added, as if trying to convince us.

"The maid served us a big roast garnished with tomatoes and hard-boiled eggs. Sylvia's husband picked up an egg and turned to Mary. 'Look,' he said, and peeled the egg in a funny way, in circles. Mary laughed. We ate quietly; we were all very tense. I looked at my watch. It was getting late. How could I have thought of the time?" Leah shouted. "This was the last time I saw my daughter! How could I possibly have thought about the time?!

"Cruel," Leah whispered to herself. "I got up from my seat and handed her over to Sylvia. 'Guard her like you would your own,' I begged her. Tears streamed down my cheeks. Sylvia came up to me. She took a white embroidered handkerchief out of her dress pocket and wiped my tears away. I held her in my arms. 'I'll take care of her,' Sylvia said. 'And we'll come to Israel as soon as you get there and settle everything.'

"The handkerchief she used to wipe away my tears that night," Leah said, "I have it with me to this very day." She pointed to the white embroidered handkerchief that she'd used as a tablecloth on the round table. "Sylvia's handkerchief saw some very difficult days with me until we made it to Israel, and afterward, too, but you, Sylvia . . . you never made it!" Leah cried, looking up toward the heavens.

"She knew," Leah continued. "She knew in her heart it would happen this way. All that property, the houses, the shops, the land . . . it seemed wrong to her to leave it all behind. Like many others, she hoped for the best.

"Before I left that night, I spoke to my Mary. 'Be a good girl,' I told her. She looked at me. And all she whispered was, 'Mama.' I never thought it would be so hard to leave her, just for a few days, maybe a few weeks. But the pain was worse than I could have imagined.

"I heard a knock on the door. My brother Jacob stood at the doorway. 'Come in,' Sylvia said. 'I've come to say goodbye,' he said, 'and to pick up my sister. We're heading out on a very long journey tonight.' 'Yes,' I said to him.

"Mary walked up to him on her little legs. 'Uncle Jacob,' she whispered. He hoisted her up in his arms and hugged her and kissed her. She played with a lock of his hair, and then he put her down and said, 'Go upstairs, child.' Then he hurried me too.

"I looked around me, to take in every detail, to remember it all. I hugged everybody again, especially Mary. I kissed her and I whispered, 'I'll see you again, my dear, in just a little while, in Israel. In the land I told you about . . . we'll pick flowers together . . . we'll eat oranges . . . do you remember?'

"Mary nodded at me. She didn't understand why everybody was sad. She followed the little girl in the white dress upstairs. 'Bye-bye,' I said.

"I left through the front door slowly, painfully. Jacob, noticing my reluctance, shut the door behind me and rushed me down the street. For a second I thought of storming back into the house, taking her back and staying in Poland. Life there was still good then, and it was a nice world to live in. When I stopped, Jacob gently whispered to me: 'I know this is hard for you. But we both know we're saving our lives, and paving the way for Sylvia, her family, and many others. And if we don't do this, there will be no one who can promise us we will ever see our loved ones again. Come, quickly. We have to hurry, or else it will be too late.'

"So I followed him," Leah whispered. "A man who was going to die. Our path to Israel was full of twists and turns. The whole time, I wondered why I was there. I thought about Mary constantly. A short time later, we learned that the war had broken out. I was terrified. I knew that Jacob had been right, that we had to hurry to do our work, create a safe place for others, and save our families. I kept hoping it was nothing but a nightmare, that I would wake up burning with a fever in my carved wooden bed at home, with Mary, Jacob, and my mother and father by my side, and my husband wiping the sweat from my forehead with a damp cloth. But no! It was a terrible reality. I was all alone on a treacherous path, on my way to a strange, distant land . . . far away from my loved ones . . . from my Mary . . . from my parents . . . and I just know they're all gone now."

"Don't say that," Dan whispered. "Maybe they're alive somewhere. Maybe you'll find them someday."

"Maybe? No. There is no maybe!" she said decisively. "I've already built enough castles made of dreams. No more. A rock has been thrown and the castle was struck. It crumbled to the ground. For months, I looked for them, and after the war I relentlessly pestered the Search Bureau for Missing Relatives.[13] I asked everyone I could about them, and finally word reached me that their house had been looted, and they were taken to a camp—a camp that no child ever came back from."

Leah stood up and brushed off her pants. She was different now, distant. "Don't pay any attention to me. I'm sorry I troubled you with the story of my past. Can I make you something to drink?"

---

13   The Search Bureau for Missing Relatives was a non-profit organization in Israel that helped Holocaust survivors locate lost relatives, friends, and acquaintances. The agency was active from 1945 to 2002.

There was no anger left in Leah's voice now, just confusion. The only trace left of her words was in her eyes, which were on fire with grief.

Without waiting for our answer, Leah walked over to the small alcove she used for a kitchen and started to make something. We could tell she was very upset, and not entirely in control. She was quick to get angry and hate herself.

A few moments later, she brought two cups of steaming tea to the table, forgetting there was nothing Dan hated more than tea.

Chapter 8

After Leah's story, I felt a strange emotion, a kind of regret about what I'd done to Miriam. Now I understood what she had gone through. Besides, she was already a part of the class—and of the kibbutz. I was one of the last ones who still ignored her, through no fault of her own. I knew I had to ask for her forgiveness, and yet a part of me felt it was beneath me, so I put off the awkward moment until nighttime.

Then at night, I'd make all sorts of excuses for myself, like that I was tired and couldn't do it properly. I'd say this to myself every night until I fell asleep. One evening I decided that I had to make it happen. So, I stayed up and planned on going to see her; but for some reason, just as I headed out, I had to go to the bathroom. After that, I went back to my bed. *Why should I wake the poor girl up from her sleep?* I thought. Yet I still felt the need to apologize to her. My heart was heavy with guilt. I got out of my bed again and went over to her bed. I felt a weird sort of coldness welling up inside me. A thousand blankets could not have warmed it. *Only Miriam's forgiveness could do it,* I told myself, and with newfound determination, I hastened my steps. But as I approached Yael's bed, which was right next to Miriam's bed, I began to slow down. However, even these tiny steps eventually brought me to Miriam's bed. Her blanket covered her up to her head, and the only sign that she was in the bed at all was her long black hair. I touched it; I'd always wanted such delicate, beautiful hair. I'd braid it during the week, and on the Sabbath, I'd let it down and weave a flower in it.

"Miriam . . ." I whispered. She was startled awake, and seeing me, of course, she was alarmed. For the first time, I noticed her eyes shooting darts. She remembered that other night when I stood by her bed, the "Night of the Purple Teddy Bear."

"I came to . . . apologize . . . to you." I pushed the words out.

She looked deep into my eyes, as if she wanted to determine if there was any truth behind my words. Seeing my pleading expression, she put a warm hand on my forehead and whispered with a sigh, "I think you've gone crazy."

"I really mean it," I said, practically begging in response to her friendly joke.

"Let's go outside," she said, sensing the awkwardness of our situation.

It truly was an odd sight: two girls, whose rivalry was known throughout the entire kibbutz, stepping out hand in hand, with blankets on their shoulders, under the moonlight. Even the moon seemed to stare at us in disbelief, and ducked behind a cloud until, convinced of my sincerity, it came back out again. We sat down on the grass, and I couldn't help but recall all the cruel pranks I'd committed, that this lawn had witnessed.

We covered ourselves in our blankets and giggled.

Abruptly, we fell silent. "I'm sorry," I whispered.

"Thank you," she said. "Let's sleep out on the lawn," she suggested quickly to spare us the awkwardness of the moment.

I nodded. We arranged our blankets, spreading mine out on the grass and using hers to cover ourselves.

We talked and laughed as if nothing bad had ever happened between us. As if we'd always been best friends.

And that's how we felt. We chatted for two hours, and there wasn't a single person on the kibbutz we didn't make a funny comment about.

"You're a real *kibbutznik* . . . you've learned how to gossip!" I laughed.

At that, Miriam suddenly went quiet.

"Are you my friend?" she asked me, gravely serious. I didn't know what to say. I wondered if she'd only been pretending, to test my sincerity. "Yes," I said. "I mean . . ."

"I just wanted to be sure that this isn't a dream, and that tomorrow we won't. . . ." She fell silent and stared at me again, studying me. Then she said, "You know, it was Rosh Hashanah."

"What?" I asked.

"The night when I was given away."

I know that many kids where given away to save their lives, but I had never met one before. I didn't know that Miriam was given away. My mind was racing with questions, but something in me told me that now was simply the time to listen, and for the first time, not to judge.

"How do you know?" I asked. "You were really little, weren't you?"

"Mama . . . well, my adoptive mama told me about it,

during the terrible, gray days of the war, when we were in the ghetto. It was *awful* over there," she emphasized. "I wouldn't wish that place on my worst enemies."

"It was that bad?" I asked, without waiting for an answer, because I'd heard the stories already, though they were hard to believe.

"Yes," she replied. "It was bad there. We lived with a few other families in one room, with one bathroom. We weren't allowed to go outside. Everyone was skinny, a frightening kind of skinny. A painful skinny. Look," she said to me. "I'm skinny, right?"

"Yes," I said. "You might be the skinniest girl in the kibbutz."

"There, everyone was much skinnier than I am. They were just bones, like half-people. They'd fall down in the street from exhaustion and hunger. And no one was allowed do a thing. Do you remember when Dan hit his head, and everyone ran over to him, worried?" I nodded. "Well, it made me remember a boy who got hurt in the ghetto by a German solider, and no one was allowed to come near him to save him. And that's how he died."

I tried to hide the look of disgust on my face.

"Are you sure I should keep telling you this?"

"Yes," I said. "Please."

"One evening, Mama woke us up. 'Get up, please, get up quickly and quietly.' I woke up. 'Mama,' I whispered. 'What's wrong?' 'You're running away,' she said, with a tear in the corner of her eye."

Miriam was teary-eyed too as she remembered this.

"'What? We're running away?' I asked her. 'Just you, children. It's bad here,' my mother said. 'It's dangerous. And I made a vow that you would go to Israel . . .' She wrapped my sister, Zipporah, and me in warm clothes, and pulled two embroidered handkerchiefs out from under the wooden plank. 'Remember us,' she said.

"Zipporah started crying. 'Mama, won't we see each other again?'

"'Let's hope so, darling. Let's hope for the best,' she told us, and hugged us tight.

"Embroidered handkerchiefs were mama's favorite. She kissed us while papa rushed us. 'Go on, children, faster.' Mama gave Zipporah our two-year-old brother, Moshe. He was sleeping soundly. She gave me a bundle packed for the road. She caressed us. 'I didn't want it to be this way,' Mama whispered, and I didn't understand why she'd said that.

"Papa led us to a fence with a hidden hole in it. Now I understood what he'd been doing for the past few days. He said, 'Run to the woods. You'll find good people there. Take care of yourselves.' We hugged one last time, and we went out through the rip in the fence. We came across a red flower. I stopped to look at it, but Zipporah urged me to move on.

"You see, Michal," Miriam explained, "the ghetto had no flowers."

"What, there were no flowers or plants at all?" I asked, shocked.

Miriam explained: "Flowers were not allowed there. Even weeds weren't; we had to rip them out, and sometimes we'd gather them up and eat them." She continued her story, and I listened. "We ran to the woods nearby. We were tired, and even though Papa had warned us not to, we rested in the shade of a tree near the ghetto. Zipporah and Moshe fell asleep. But I stayed awake and thought about Mama and Papa, who'd stayed behind in the ghetto.

"When morning came, the sun was bright and warm. Zipporah and Moshe were still fast asleep. I saw that people were stepping out of their houses in the ghetto.

The ones who resisted were beaten by German soldiers and fell to the ground. Suddenly I saw that my mother and father were also in the group. They were led right by us, and Papa tried pushing Mama into the woods to save her, but he didn't see that a German soldier had noticed them. When she tried to run, he shot her.

"Mama fell on the path, so close to us. If only she'd looked up, she would have noticed us; we were just a few feet away. I wanted to come out of my hiding spot, to pull her into the woods with us. Papa lingered there too; he tried to hoist her on his shoulders, but the soldier began to whip him. Papa didn't give up. He looked up, and then he saw me. He was frightened for us. His eyes were pleading with me not to come out, to stay in the woods. The soldier kept beating him and dragging him along. Mama was left on the path.

"After the convoy passed, I came out of my hiding spot. I walked over to my mother, who was bleeding on the ground. She recognized me, though she was barely conscious, her mind in a fog. 'Miriam,' she whispered. 'Don't tell your brother and sister about this . . . take care of Zipporah and Moshe . . . and take my bundle. It's under my coat.'

"'Mama,' I sobbed quietly. 'Don't die. Please . . .'

"'Child,' she said to me. 'In a few moments, more cruel German soldiers will get here, and they'll catch you. Please, run for your lives. You can't help me any longer.' Then she rested her head on the ground. After mumbling a few more words, my mother died."

I looked at Miriam. Her haggard features paled, and she put her hand on her heart, over the pocket of her pajama top. Her moan-like breaths reminded me of Leah telling her story.

"Calm down," I whispered. "Please, stop." But she needed to keep going. I put my hand on her shoulder.

"I hid," she said. "I waited, and another group of Jews from the ghetto were led by. They, too, were beaten and dragged away. Some of them fell down on the path. I wanted to take my mother's body away from there, and fast, so that Moshe and Zipporah wouldn't see her. I wanted them to keep thinking what I had thought before this morning, that the people of the ghetto would eventually be set free, that it was some sort of unjust prison. That's what Papa used to say to us. He may have believed it himself, that the war would end soon. I dragged Mama behind me, far off the path."

"Wasn't it hard for you to do that?" I asked, my voice full of admiration.

"Michal," she said, "in times like that, you don't think about what's hard, but about what's necessary. I spent an hour digging a grave with my bare hands under a tree. It wasn't that deep, but at least Mama got a grave—she was the only one. I carved the word MAMA into the tree above it. I said a prayer, and I went back to Zipporah and Moshe, carrying with me the belongings and jewelry that were in Mama's coat. I stashed them deep in our bundle. 'Zipporah, get up,' I tried rocking my sister awake. 'It's morning, and we have to leave this place. It's dangerous here.'

"'Okay,' she said, and sat up, stretching. 'I'll take Moshe,' I said, wanting to help. I carried him in my arms, and we walked deep into the woods, not knowing where we were headed, or what tomorrow would bring. We walked during the day. In the afternoon, we gathered twigs for a fire. At night we sat by the fire and tried to sleep on an empty stomach. Zipporah often complained that we'd had more food in the ghetto, and that Mama and Papa had probably gone back to their house and become rich again, while we wandered through the woods, starving.

"It hurt me to hear Zipporah talk about our parents that way. *Who knows where Papa is now?* I thought to myself, and resolved to keep the horrible secret of what I'd seen happen to Mama and Papa locked in my heart.

"Sometimes, when the hunger got worse, if we were near a village or town, I'd sell a piece of Mama's jewelry, even though that put us in danger of being discovered. Sometimes, Zipporah refused to eat, claiming she wasn't hungry, but I knew she was doing it to save food for us. Sometimes, wandering through the woods, we'd come across other children; we'd travel with them for a few days and then part ways. We met adults, too, but it was dangerous to move in large groups, so they preferred to stay alone and told us to try our luck in the villages, with kindhearted farmers.

"One day, it was Zipporah's turn to carry Moshe in her arms. He'd grown and started walking faster on his own by this point, which made things easier, but he still walked very slowly. He was, after all, just a little boy. We were walking in the woods, as usual, when suddenly we arrived at a road where Nazi vehicles were passing. We had no compass and no map, so instead of going straight we'd accidentally veered off toward the road.

"We hid among the trees immediately and wanted to run back into the woods, which had a thicker cover of trees. But then, Moshe mumbled something. I think he asked for water or food, something basic that every baby boy should be able to ask for—unless he is a hunted Jewish baby. A soldier sitting in one of the cars noticed us and called to his friends to shoot at us. We ran. Zipporah held on tightly to Moshe. The soldier and his friends began chasing us. Their guns and rifles were aimed at us. They fired.

"Michal," Miriam turned to me. "I felt like a rabbit in one of Papa's hunting trips. The soldier fired, and everything went black. But I wasn't the one who'd been hit. Zipporah was shot in her shoulder. I was terrified. 'Keep going!' I screamed at her. 'Take Moshe,' she said, groaning in pain. Even then, she still tried to hide her pain from me. I took Moshe, who cried in my arms, and we kept running. The soldier fired again. This time he hit her in the middle of the back, and she went down. I knew she was dead, but there was no time to cry for my sister, so I ran even faster. The bullets whistled over our heads, but somehow we were able to escape them."

I was so immersed in Miriam's story that I hadn't

noticed I'd been holding my breath out of fear for their lives. And now, at once, I let the air out of my lungs in a sigh of relief. Miriam glanced at me and continued her story.

"I didn't know, and I still don't know how long we were in the woods. One cold, gray morning, Moshe and I were sitting in our hiding spot. We knew we were deep into the woods, and we didn't want to move anywhere. That day, a girl approached us. She'd walked into the woods so quietly that we hadn't even noticed her.

"'Hello,' she said to us.

"'Hello,' I answered, frightened. She didn't look like one of 'us,' the children who'd escaped.

"'Those clothes are small on you,' she said to me.

"You have to understand that until then I had paid no attention to it, and now, suddenly, I noticed how worn and torn our clothes were.

"'Come,' the girl said to me.

"She came closer and repeated what she'd said: 'Come over to our house to eat.' I was afraid of her, but we were so tired of running that I said yes.

"The girl's mother was alarmed by the sight of us, and she took us into her home with great apprehension. The mother and daughter exchanged a few words in secret, while the mother set the table for us. 'Eat,' she urged us. We ate soup and meat. It was the best food I ever had in my life," Miriam said, smacking her lips, as if she were eating delicacies at that very moment.

"After that, the woman bathed us and dressed us in her children's clothes. She agreed to let us live with her 'for a short time.' I remember her emphasizing that.

"While we stayed there, I milked the cow for her and gathered wood for the furnace. We lived with that Polish family for a relatively long time, until one day I sensed something strange about the mother's behavior. I asked her about it, and she told me we had to leave because the Germans were closing in on their town.

"We packed our few belongings, and the woman sent us off with a large piece of meat and a small cloth sack with milk. Moshe didn't understand what was going on or why we had to leave. I couldn't explain it to him.

"'Leave this place,' the woman said as she rushed us and shoved us out the front gate. And so, Michal, we kept wandering through the woods. Now and then I sold another piece of Mama's jewelry, until only one was left. She had always worn it on her finger."

As she said this, Miriam pulled the ring out of an inner pocket on her pajamas. "I always keep it with me," she said, and slipped the beautiful ring onto her finger. "My mother had beautiful hands." I stared, a little jealously, at the sight of the red studded ring.

"After several weeks of wandering, we met a group of kind Jews and fighters. They were called Partisans, and they tried to take revenge on the Nazis. We stayed in the woods with them until the war ended. The Jews were gathered in a special camp where they fed us and gave us warm clothes. They took good care of us. We stayed in that camp for a few weeks, and a rumor started spreading that the Jews were going to the land of Israel. A lot of Jews wanted to come to Israel, but many weren't allowed to go, or they couldn't get the proper paperwork; so, they just gathered up the children.

"They dressed us in all white, just like Mama used to for special occasions. The ship that was going to bring us to Israel had docked in the port that night. Many people without permits tried to board it and stow away. In the morning, we children boarded the ship. It was very crowded on the deck, but we didn't feel it. Many of us, and the adults, too, caught terrible diseases and got really sick. The voyage was hard, and my pristine clothes became filthy and gray. And that's how I arrived in the land of Israel, and at the kibbutz."

I went silent. I didn't know how to react to the story of a little girl's wandering with her toddler brother. The only question that popped into my mind was, "So how did you know how to solve the problem in the math quiz?"

She smiled. "While we were in the refugee camp, waiting for our papers to come through so we could go to Israel, I met a man who became like a father to me. And he was the one who taught me to read and write, and to do math too. He said it was unthinkable that I should come to the land of our forefathers without knowing how to write my own name. If only he knew how much he'd helped me. . . ." she said and winked at me.

I hugged her warmly and whispered, "It's good that you came. . . . I don't know how I could have treated you the way I did! Will you forgive me?" I whispered, pleading.

"I've already forgiven you," she said.

Our eyelids fell like curtains on the past.

Chapter 9

"Good morning," Leah called out to us with glee. "Have you two reached a truce? Excellent!" She smiled at us. "Come in, it's late," she added, and turned to go wake the other children.

"Leah," I turned to her. "Hold on. Look at this," I said, and held out Miriam's hand, wearing the gold ring studded with a red precious stone on her finger.

"This is the only souvenir she has left of her mother." I added quickly, now well versed in the story of Miriam's life and proud of it.

Leah stepped closer to Miriam, a look of shock in her eyes. She held her hand tightly and stared at the ring and at Miriam. "Where did you find that?" she said, with great difficulty.

"Mama gave it to me before she died," Miriam said, a bit surprised by Leah's reaction.

"Sylvia? *Was Sylvia your mother?!*"

"You knew my mother?" Miriam asked, stunned.

"Mary! My Mary! My darling daughter!" Leah hugged Miriam, and tears flooded her soft eyes.

Miriam responded, "You . . . you're my real mother?"

"Yes, my darling girl, yes!" They hugged. "You're . . . here . . . I never even thought of it!" Leah mumbled through her tears.

They cried tears of joy, which flowed down their cheeks. My eyes filled with tears too, and I joined their hug.

Hearing the cries of joy, everybody came out of their rooms and watched the emotional reunion on the lawn.

Manek stepped closer as well, and said with a smile: "Truly, a great Hanukkah miracle happened here too."

Acknowledgments

To Guy, the love of my life, my rock, my everything, for believing in me, getting this book translated, and encouraging me to bring it to light.

To Kari and Eytan, Mom & Dad, who believed a 11-year-old could write something worth publishing, and for teaching me that together we can do anything. Everything I have ever achieved is because of that and you. I love you.

To Yael Baruch, who saw the potential in me, and published this book in Hebrew in Israel in 1987.

To Jason Schneider, RIP, who said: "This is the book I want to publish." We have never met, but you were a truly great friend to me.

To Jessica Burch, my editor, who has been smart, and patient, and creative. You are truly wonderful. Thank you!